Polarity Bear Tours the Zoo
A Central Park Adventure

For Penelope Bareau

© 2011 by Sue de Cuevas
Illustrations © 2011 by Wendy Rasmussen

Printed in the United States of America

First Printing, 2011

ISBN 978-0-692-01552-0

Polarity Bear Books
5 River Road, Suite 234
Wilton, CT 06897

www.polaritybearbooks.com

Polarity Bear Tours the Zoo
A Central Park Adventure

Sue de Cuevas

Illustrated by
Wendy Rasmussen

A polar bear lived in the Central Park Zoo
Whose color was white but whose feelings were blue,
Who stood in a corner and looked with a sigh
At all of the visitors wandering by,
And cried, "I have nothing to do!

"Here I stand in my cage at the Central Park Zoo,

And I watch all the children as they wander through.

When they look at me, what do they see?

Only poor Polarity,

The bear who has nothing to do!"

One summery evening, when no one was there,

Except for the white-coated, blue-mooded bear,

She stuck out her tongue and said, "Phoo!

I wish I had something to do!"

And do you know what happened?

Her tongue hit the bar

(It actually did, since it stuck out so far)

And went through:

It broke the bar in two!

The bear stared at the bar, and then

She stuck her tongue way out again.

Another bar was torn away,

And then a third, and then – Hurray!

The bars were down. The bear was free

To take a holiday.

"Where shall I go? What shall I do?

I'm free to roam around the zoo!

What's over here? What's over there?

Surprises for a polar bear

And all the fun I've waited for.

Hot Icicles! I'll go explore!"

There's a pool, deep and wide, where the sea lions glide
Past the people who lean on the rail.
But on that day, one guest would not stay with the rest –
A guest who had paws and a tail!

"Hello," said the bear as she perched on the rim.
"It's wonderful watching you sea lions swim.
I hope you'll permit me to follow your lead.
A bear in your lair may be just what you need!"

A splish! a splash! and in she went,
Crying, "This is excellent!"

Then with a grunt (a happy sound)

She started swimming round and round,

Till all at once, she found her tail

Had turned into a mini-sail,

Up-ended – like her paddling paws –

A foot above a sea lion's jaws.

But not for long, for down she came,

Then up. The sea lions played their game.

What game? Well, what do you suppose?

Bounce the bear from nose to nose!

A dozen times the bouncing bear

Went tumbling through the summer air.

A dozen times, and once again,

She bounced across the watery pen.

"Stop! stop!" she cried. "What's fun for you

Is turning me all black and blue!"

But zing – and zoom – just like a ball,

Around she went and went, till all

At once, with a colossal zing,

The white bear bounced beyond the ring.

Then down she sat and rubbed her tail.

"Hot Icicles! How did I fail?

I only wanted fun. Now they

Have black-and-blued my holiday.

Goodbye, sea lions. I'm going now."

She left them with a little bow.

Polarity roamed through the Central Park Zoo,

Seeking and searching for something to do.

She said "hi" to the monkeys and "tweet" to the birds,

But though she spoke with friendly words

She didn't stop. Then suddenly –

What's this new possibility?

A goat, a bear, a kangaroo,

An elephant, a penguin too,

A hippopotamus whose chin

Rests lightly on a violin,

Two monkeys sitting by a gong;

And all this playing, dancing throng

Has an important job to do:

To tell the time the whole day through.

Each half-hour, through the day,

They start to prance – they start to play.

Around and round they go, and then

They wait till they can start again.

Polarity beamed at the Delacorte Clock.

"What a splendid surprise! What a fabulous flock!

I'm going to join them. I'm going to prance!

I'll turn when they turn. I'll dance when they dance!

I'll spin on one leg through the air

Exactly like that other bear!"

Polarity began to climb,

Resolved to dance her way through time.

Up she clambered brick by brick,

Not too slowly, not too quick,

Until at last she'd joined the flock

Of animals upon the clock.

It was very quiet for a while.

Then the bear began to smile

As "Bong, bong, bong," the bells rang out,

For soon, she knew, she'd dance about.

But then her smile began to fade,

For what a noise those great bells made!

This close to her, the chimes, resounding,

Set the poor bear's ears a-pounding.

But trying still to do her best,

She started dancing with the rest.

With hands on ears to stop the din,

With one foot up, with half a grin,

The polar bear began to spin.

And spin she did, till halfway through

She lost her step and down she flew!

Down! Past clock and flock and all.

Down! No chance to stop her fall.

Down! She landed in a ball

Upon the ground, and with a sigh

She sadly said, "Dear clock, goodbye!"

Polarity roamed through the Central Park Zoo,

Seeking and searching for something to do.

Past trees and through bushes she went, on the run,

Eager to add to her holiday fun,

Till with a bound, a leap, a yell,

She stopped before the Carousel.

Gleaming horses, eyes alight,

Painted brown and black and white,

Painted for a bear's delight!

In the corner, looking down,

There's a happy, laughing clown.

There's another – there's a third.

The bear looked up and said, "My word!

Start the music! Get in gear!

Polarity the bear is here!"

But no one had a word to say.

The Carousel was closed that day.

Polarity rode anyway.

She leaped the gate to get inside.

She knew that she'd know how to ride.

She pulled the lever. "All aboard,"

She shouted to the horsey horde.

"I'll saddle up. I'll have my fun.

You – big brown horse – you're just the one.

Hot Icicles! I'll mount your back.

You other horses, clear the track!"

Around and around went Polarity Bear,

Gliding along through the summery air.

Her blue mood was rosy, her face wore a smile,

As round and around she went, mile after mile.

Mile after mile? But that's quite a long trip

For a bear feeling dizzy and likely to slip.

"Enough of this music! Stop, horsey, please! Whoa!

How much longer must I go

Around and round? Until I drop?"

But the horses wouldn't stop.

Someone had to throw the switch

That slows them from their frantic pitch;

But who? For not a soul was there

Except a very dizzy bear.

"Help!" the bear began to yell,

"Won't someone stop this Carousel?"

Dizzily, she stumbled down,

Bumping horses, black and brown:

"Hot Icicles! I'm bruised, I'm shaken!

What an endless ride I've taken."

Finally she stumbled clear,

Stopped the music, locked the gear,

And softly said, "Goodbye, my dear."

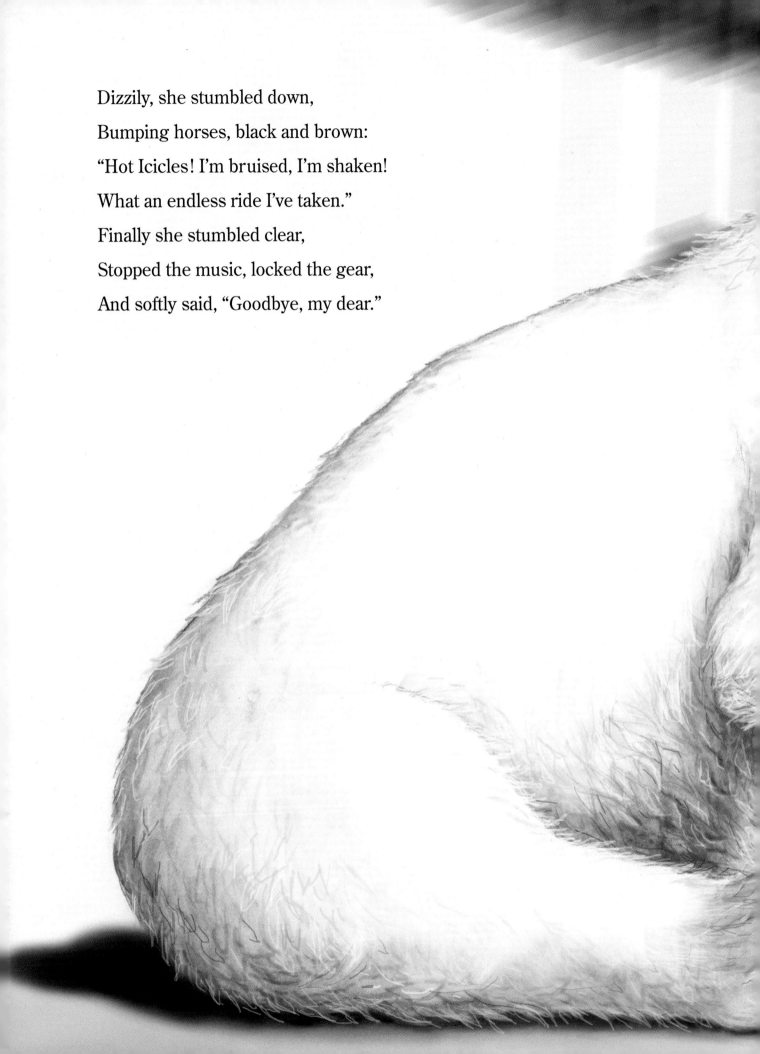

Polarity ran through the Central Park Zoo,

Knowing exactly the right thing to do.

Back to her cage she went, lickety-split,

Pulled open the bars that her black tongue had slit,

And leaped back inside them, and shut them up tight.

Then, looking around her, she said with delight:

"I'm glad to be back where I started this poem!
It may look like a cage, but it's mine, and it's home.
I'll smile at the children. They'll smile at me.
I'll splash in my own pool and climb my own tree.
And whenever I'm blue, I'll remember this day.
I went out. I came back. Now I'm ready to stay."

At that moment, like magic, a little man came

From a Zookeeper's truck with a note in a frame.

He read it out loud. Why don't you do the same?

Calling all bears in the Central Park Zoo!

Hear what the management's going to do!
We're removing the bars from your tight little cages.
We'll fix up your quarters (in slow, easy stages).
We'll give you new trees,
We'll make everything pretty —
You'll hardly suppose that you're here in the city.
We do want to please you.
We don't want to bore you.
Polarity Bear, we'll do anything for you!

Today, if you go to the Central Park Zoo,

If you're one of the visitors wandering through,

You can visit a creature whose color is white

While her feelings are rosy from morning to night.

She seems so contented, you'd scarcely believe

That Polarity Bear was once anxious to leave.

(But maybe someday – who knows when –
She'll take a holiday again.)